Lulu's Busy Day

To Auntie Esther with love

ORCHARD BOOKS
338 Euston Road, London NW1 3BH
Orchard Books Australia
Level 17/207 Kent Street, Sydney, NSW 2000

First published in 2000 by Orchard Books
First published in paperback in 2001
This edition published in 2009
ISBN 978 1 40830 340 5
Text and illustrations © Caroline Uff 2000

1 3 5 7 9 10 8 6 4 2

Printed in China

Orchard Books is a division of Hachette Children's Books, an Hachette Livre UK company.
www.hachettelivre.co.uk

Lulu's Busy Day

Caroline Uff

ORCHARD BOOKS

Hello Lulu.

What are you doing today?

Lulu is busy drawing.
What a beautiful picture.

Lulu likes playing ball.
Catch,
Lulu!

Lulu is off to the park. She wears her new bobbly hat.

Look what Lulu finds...

Lulu is being
a duck.

Pit pat
quack
quack.

High high, up in the sky.

Lulu loves swinging with her best friend.

What lovely big
puddles.

Splish
splash
splosh!

It's time to go home now.

"Bye bye,"
says
Lulu.

Lulu loves teatime.
Yum yum.

Lulu builds houses
and big castles.

"Crash!" says Lulu. All fall down.

Time to
tidy up now, Lulu.

Lulu likes lots and lots
of bubbles in her bath.

Open wide, Teddy.
Let's brush your teeth.

Lulu snuggles down
for a bedtime story.

Shhh!
Lulu is fast asleep.

Night night Lulu.